Belinda
the Beetle

Susan and John are thrilled when
their parents buy Belinda, the little
red Volkswagen Beetle. But then
Belinda is stolen by a gang of jewel
thieves – what do they want?

**Also by the same author,
and available in Knight Books:**

BELINDA BEATS THE BAND

Belinda the Beetle

REV W AWDRY

Illustrated by Val Biro

KNIGHT BOOKS
Hodder and Stoughton

Text copyright © 1958, 1992 by Rev. W. Awdry

Illustrations copyright © 1992 by Val Biro

First published in Great Britain in hardback in 1958 by Brockhampton Press Ltd

Knight Books edition 1992

Printed and bound in Great Britain for Hodder and Stoughton Children's Books a division of Hodder and Stoughton Ltd., Mill Road, Dunton Green, Sevenoaks, Kent TN13 2YA. (Editorial Office: 47 Bedford Square, London WC1B 3DP) by Clays Ltd, St Ives plc. Typeset by Rowland Phototypesetting Ltd., Bury St Edmunds, Suffolk.

British Library CIP

A Catalogue record for this book is available from the British Library

ISBN 0-340-58006-2

Contents

1 Snoop by name

Mr William Whisker finished his breakfast, and came down to open the showroom. He pushed up the shutters, and unlocked the door. Then, in the morning light he looked at his cars.

There were Maisie the Minx, Jacky the Jaguar, and Susie the Snipe. He went to each and stroked their gleaming paint. He thought how much he loved them, and how he hated having to sell them.

He sometimes talked about it to his wife. Mrs Whisker was a large woman with no sentiment. 'I don't like parting with them and that's a fact,' he would say. 'How do I know that they are going to good homes?'

'Rubbish, William!' Mrs Whisker would

answer. 'If you don't sell your cars, what will you do for bread and butter?'

Poor Mr Whisker had no answer to that. He was very fond of bread and butter. He had it for breakfast, and supper, and tea; he even had it sometimes for elevenses.

He looked at his cars and wondered which of them would have to go today. 'Jacky's spoken for, and so is Maisie, and someone came in to look at Susie yesterday. One good thing,' he thought, 'I shan't lose Belinda. No one will want to buy her.' And he went over to the corner where she stood, and stroked her lovingly.

Belinda was a little Volkswagen Beetle with a soft top. She was painted red, and her number was BLN 111.

Mr Whisker was fond of Belinda. He was sorry for her too. She had had an accident with a lorry, and had never been the same car since. Another garage had tried to mend her, but she would never go properly. Her master soon got tired of trying to make her start. He bought a new car from Mr Whisker and gave him Belinda in part exchange.

Mr Whisker talked to Belinda. He coaxed Belinda. He took off his coat and did all sorts of things to her engine, which was at the back end. Belinda liked Mr Whisker, and tried hard to please him, but she didn't feel well, and no

matter how much she tried, her engine kept
stopping.

'Whew!' said Mr Whisker at last, and wiped his
face with a large spotted handkerchief. 'I'm hot!
It's no good, Belinda, I can't put you right. We'll
have to see what George can do. Come along.'

He pushed her through the door in the back of
the shop to the shed where George Egg worked.

George Egg was one of the friendliest men you
could meet – everyone called him George, even
the local children. He was a large round man

with a red, smiling face. At least, his face was always red and smiling when he came to work in the morning, but though it was still smiling, it was generally black with oil by the time he went home. George loved cars, and his shed was a kind of car hospital. When anybody had a car that was out of order, they brought it to George, and George put it right. He would open the bonnet and look inside. He would take parts out and put them back again, and lo and behold, the car would be as good as new.

People would say that George did it by magic but George only laughed. 'It's quite simple,' he would tell them, 'when you know what to do. It's knowing what to do that counts.'

William Whisker pushed Belinda over to George. He hoped that George would know what to do with her.

George took Belinda's engine to pieces. Belinda didn't like that. She was afraid that George might lose some of her parts.

'What would become of me then?' she thought sadly.

But George was very gentle with her. 'It's all right, my pretty,' he said reassuringly. 'I shan't lose any of your parts. We'll clean them and mend them, and put them back again, and then you'll be as good as new.'

George couldn't work on Belinda all the time,

4

because people kept bringing cars for him to mend; but he was very careful of Belinda's parts.

He wedged a tray on top of her engine, and put her parts tidily on the tray. He wrote a notice in large letters, PLEASE DO NOT TOUCH.

'Thank you, George,' said Belinda. 'That is nice. They won't get lost now.'

Presently a man brought an old car in for George to mend. Belinda saw George open its bonnet and look inside.

'That won't take long,' he said cheerfully.

'I'll wait,' said the man whose name was Mr Snoop. He started looking round the shed. Belinda watched him. He had thick eyebrows, a sharp face, and wore a hat. A cigarette drooped from his mouth. Belinda didn't like the look of him at all. 'I hope he doesn't come near me,' she said.

But that's just what Mr Snoop did.

He walked all round the shed with his hands in his pockets, staring at the other cars, and last of all he came to Belinda. He looked at Belinda. He made Belinda feel creepy.

He waited till George wasn't looking. He opened Belinda's door and poked about inside. He prodded her cushions.

'Ooooh!' shuddered Belinda. 'This is dreadful.'

Mr Snoop went round to the back, and saw Belinda's parts neatly arranged on her tray. Her

5

engine lid was held up by a metal prop. George had not fastened it firmly. Mr Snoop made sure that George wasn't looking, and poked his head under Belinda's engine lid. Ash from his cigarette fell all over.

'What a cheek,' thought Belinda crossly. 'I'll pay him out.'

Mr Snoop picked up one of her parts. 'Don't touch,' said Belinda. She gave a little jerk, the

prop fell away and her engine lid fell down clang on Mr Snoop's head.

'I've got you!' chuckled Belinda. 'Serves you right. Just you wait till George comes.'

George heard the clang, and saw Snoop caught in Belinda's engine lid. 'Here, you, come out of that,' he shouted.

Snoop lifted Belinda's engine lid and turned to face George. George's face was red, but he wasn't smiling. He was very cross.

'There's a notice saying "Don't Touch". Can't you read?'

'I wasn't doing any harm, mister,' said Snoop. 'Just having a look round.'

George lifted the engine lid. Belinda's parts were disarranged, they were covered in cigarette ash, the tool-bag was open and the tools all over the tray.

'Take your car and go,' he ordered. 'Snoop by name and Snoop by nature. We don't want your sort here.'

Snoop slouched to his car and drove away.

'Well done, Belinda!' said George. 'You caught him nicely. He'd have taken some of your parts, I shouldn't wonder, and put them in his old car.'

'What a horrid man!' said Belinda shuddering.

'Never mind, Belinda, he's gone. Now we'll put you right.'

He cleaned Belinda's parts all over again and put them back in her inside.

'Thank you, George, that's better,' she said comfortably.

George started her engine and she hummed him a little song. Mr Whisker came in. 'I'm better now,' she sang happily. George stood listening with his head on one side.

'She's better, William,' he said, 'but she's not right yet. I'll leave her running for a little to get warmed up. Then I'll take her out. Would you like that, Belinda?'

'Yes please, George,' she answered.

George tidied up, then he squeezed into the driving seat.

'Come on, Belinda, let's go,' and away they went.

They had a nice run through the town and back again. Neither Belinda nor George noticed Mr Snoop draw back into a doorway in the High Street as they passed. He was talking to a man in a brown suit.

2   Not for sale

That afternoon the man in the brown suit walked along Pump Street. He looked rich and respectable. His brown suit was neat and new. He wore a smart trilby hat. His tie was fastened with a gold pin. His brown shoes looked expensive and well-polished, and he carried a leather brief-case.

He looked at the cars parked end to end along the street. No one was about, and he strolled up to the best, a big Bentley. He opened the door, got in and drove away.

Now if I tell you that the car did not belong to him, you will know what sort of a man he was. He was not respectable at all. He was a thief. He called himself Mr Brown, but that wasn't his real name. He had a great many names. Whenever he went to a different place he used a different one. He did that to make it hard for the police to catch him.

He drove to the garage, and walked into the showroom. Mr Whisker came to meet him.

'I want a small car for my wife,' said Brown. 'Have you anything that might suit?'

'I'm sorry, sir, I've nothing suitable in stock, but if you would take these catalogues, your wife could choose the car she likes, and I should be very pleased to get it for you.'

'That would not do at all,' said Brown. 'It is to be a surprise for her. I want it at once. A second-hand car would do.'

Brown had been walking about the room as he talked. Now he stood looking through the open door into George's workshop. 'I see you have a little Beetle there,' he said carelessly. 'That might suit. May I see it, please?'

Mr Whisker took him through. George was working on Belinda. Brown went all round her, lifted her engine lid, poked her cushions and fiddled with her controls.

'Oh dear!' thought Belinda. 'I don't like him at all.' It was all she could do to keep still while he poked her about.

'Oh! Oh! Ooooh!' she cried, as he tried the horn.

'Yes,' said Brown thoughtfully. 'This will do very well. How much?'

Belinda felt dreadful. 'Oh dear!' she said to herself, 'he wants to buy me.'

Mr Whisker was taken aback. 'Er, what did you say, sir?'

'I said "How much?"' snapped Brown. 'How much do you want for this car?'

'But surely, sir,' said Mr Whisker, 'you know your own business best, of course, but this car would be most unsuitable as a present for your wife. It's being repaired after an accident, and isn't in good condition. Wouldn't your wife prefer a new car of this sort? I could get one through for you very quickly.'

'No, no, no, no!' said Brown. 'A new car would not do at all. My wife is, shall we say, a careless driver. She has not yet passed her test, and I can't afford to have her damaging a new car, but an old one like this wouldn't matter a bit. How much?'

'Worse and worse!' thought Belinda. She felt as if her engine had sunk to her wheels. She looked anxiously at Mr Whisker. 'Don't sell me! Please don't sell me,' she whispered.

'Poor Belinda!' thought Mr Whisker. 'He wants to buy her for his wife who can't drive, and he says it wouldn't matter if she gets damaged.' Aloud he said, 'I'm sorry, sir, but this car is not for sale.'

'Rubbish man!' said Brown. 'Here's £1,000.'

'No, sir.'

'£1,500 then.'

'No, sir, I really cannot.'

'£2,000, money down.' And Brown rummaged in his brief-case and produced a wad of notes.

'No, sir, I'm sorry, but I wouldn't sell you the car even if you offered me £3,000. For one thing, my mechanic hasn't finished repairing her yet, and I make it a rule never to sell a defective car to anybody. It isn't fair to my customers, besides being bad business, and for another thing, it isn't fair to the car to sell her to someone who's likely to damage her.'

Brown turned on his heel and went out. 'I never heard such nonsense!' he stormed angrily. 'Not fair to the car indeed. A car's only a machine.'

'That's all *you* know about it,' said Mr Whisker, as he closed the door behind him.

'Whew!' said William Whisker. He came through into George's workshop and sat down.

'Thank you, Mr Whisker,' whispered Belinda.

Mr Whisker didn't hear her, he was too exhausted. 'Have you any more tea in that pot, George?' he asked. 'I could do with some just now.'

'Certainly, William, if you don't mind using my cup,' and he poured out the tea, steaming hot.

Mr Whisker drank it gratefully. George picked up his tools and started work on Belinda again.

'You know, William,' said George after a while, 'I admired the way you stood up to that chap. Fancy saying it wouldn't matter if Belinda was damaged! And when you said "No" to £2,000, I wanted to get up and cheer. Belinda was excited, weren't you, old girl?'

'Yes, George, I was,' and she gave a wriggle at the thought.

'Of course you were. Keep still, can't you? How can I mend you if you make your bits slip out of my fingers like this? That's the third time I've had to crawl underneath and pick up this washer.'

'You're tickling, George.'

'Tickling, my foot!' grunted George. 'You're wriggling, Belinda, that's what. Look here! That's the fourth time that washer's slipped! If you move again, Belinda, I'll . . . I'll chock your wheels!'

At this dreadful threat, Belinda subsided and George was able to continue his work, watched by William.

'You know, George,' he said at last, 'quite apart from saying he didn't mind if Belinda was damaged, I didn't like that Brown.'

'He was a wrong 'un all right. Did you notice how he never looked you straight in the face when he was talking?'

'No more he did, now I come to think of it.'

'All that tale, too, of wanting to give his wife a present. I don't believe he's got a wife. I know that if I was as well off as he makes out to be, and I gave my wife a present of an old car like Belinda, why, she'd go up in smoke!'

Belinda's engine lid shut with a bang. 'Here, Belinda,' protested George, 'you nearly nipped me then.'

Next he heard Belinda making a most peculiar noise. Have you ever heard a motor car crying? You haven't? Then I can't explain what it was like, because there's no other noise like it.

'What's the matter, Belinda?' asked William.

'Ge-Ge-Ge-George said I was an old car and his w-w-wife w-w-w-w-wouldn't like me as a present.'

'Oh dear!' said George. 'I'm sorry, Belinda, I didn't mean to hurt your feelings. I meant that if I was as rich and stuck up as that Brown, my wife would be stuck up too, and she wouldn't like a dear old car like you. You don't want to be a present for Mrs Brown, now do you?'

'N-n-n-no!'

'Mr Whisker and I think that Brown is a bad man, and he's telling us lies. We didn't mean that you were a horrid old car and no use to anybody. You're a very nice car, and we want you to have a good home.'

'Y-y-yes, George.'

'Well then, give over crying, there's a good car, and let me get on with mending you. I can't mend you if you go on hiccoughing like that.'

'Yes, George, I'll try.'

George worked in silence for a while. Then, 'It's funny, William,' he said, 'but Brown is the second bad type we've had interested in Belinda today,' and he told him what Snoop had tried to do that morning.

'Did you notice Brown poking about inside? It seemed to me as if he was looking for something. No ordinary customer puts his fingers down the cracks beside the cushions. Brown did.'

'Snoop was looking for something inside Belinda this morning. He thought I wasn't watching him, but I was.'

'Did he find anything, George?'

'No, not a thing. I should have been on to him if he had.'

'They were both looking for something and they didn't find it,' said Mr Whisker thoughtfully. 'Let's have a go ourselves, shall we?

Belinda, we think you've got something hidden inside you and we're going to look for it.'

'What is it?' asked Belinda.

'Search me,' said George, 'but it must be valuable, otherwise Brown wouldn't have offered £2,000 for you this afternoon.'

George and William searched Belinda thoroughly. They took out the cushions and looked underneath them. They looked in every possible hiding place they could think of. They even took the tyre off the spare wheel to see if anything was hidden there. But they didn't find anything except dust.

'There can't be anything,' said William at last. 'All the same, I don't like it. Look here, George, drop everything else and get Belinda finished, and I'll try and find a good home for her before those two jokers come snooping again.'

3 The new owners

Next morning Mr Whisker was worried. He had finished his elevenses and still he hadn't been able to think of anybody who might want Belinda and give her a good home.

He went to the door and looked up and down the street. He was just turning back to the shop when he saw the Vicar of Arlstead and his family coming along.

First came Susan, hop-skip-and-jumping. She looked excited about something.

Susan was ten. She had pig-tails, a round face, a broad grin, and a long tongue.

Her brother John came behind. He was eight, and smaller, slower and dreamier than Susan, but he was a very solid little boy. He adored

18

Susan, though he didn't let her boss him.

'Wait for me, Susan,' he called.

'We can't wait,' Susan called back. 'It might be gone if we don't hurry. Oh, I do wish Mummy and Daddy would be quick,' and she looked back and saw them passing the bus station some way behind. They were walking arm in arm and trying to look unconcerned. 'But really,' thought Mr Whisker, 'they look as excited as the children! What's up, I wonder?'

He hadn't long to wait.

Susan skipped along the pavement, turned her head to look at John, tripped over her feet and fell into Mr Whisker's arms.

'Hold up, Susan!' he said, and held her out at arm's length, to make sure there was no damage.

'Oh, Mr Whisker, it's so exciting. Daddy had some money this morning. He lent it to someone ages and ages ago and it never came back and he forgot all about it, and then it came back this morning, and we want to buy a little car for all of us, a little red car like George was in yesterday morning. You have still got it, Mr Whisker, haven't you? Oh, do please say you have,' and she stopped quite out of breath.

'Well, I never did!' said Mr Whisker, and he was so surprised and pleased that he didn't know what to say.

'You've still got it, haven't you, Mr Whisker?' John's face was looking anxiously up at him now.

'Yes, I've still got it,' he smiled.

'Oh, goody goody,' and the children did a dance round Mr Whisker in front of the shop. 'Then we *can* buy it. Please, Mr Whisker, *do* say we can.'

'Here, half a minute, half a minute. Stop jigetting, can't you? You're making me feel quite giddy,' and Mr Whisker reached out and caught a wriggling, laughing child with each hand. 'Let's wait until your dad and mum arrive, then we'll see what it's all about.'

'Good morning, Mrs Exel. Good morning, Vicar.'

'How are you, William?'

'Nicely, thank you.'

Susan could bear it no longer. She tugged at her father's hand excitedly. 'Mr Whisker's got it, Daddy,' she whispered.

The Vicar smiled. 'Well, William,' he said. 'I expect Susan's told you all about it. I had a windfall this morning, and we want to spend some of it on a little car. Susan says she saw George in a little red one yesterday morning. Have you still got it, and, if so, do you think it would suit us?'

Mr Whisker smiled at the family's eager faces. 'I think she might,' he said. 'Come and see.' So they all filed through to where George was giving finishing touches to Belinda's engine.

'Morning, Vicar,' said George, looking up. 'What can I do for you?'

'Morning, George, we've come to see this little car. Do you think we could all fit in her, or are we too big?'

George twinkled. He pretended to consider. 'Well, Vicar, you and Mrs Exel will fit in the front seats nicely, no trouble at all, and so will John in the back, but I'm bothered about Susan,' and here he gave a large wink. 'If her legs get any longer she'll have to put them over the side!'

Everybody laughed, and Susan made a face at George, but she didn't really mind. George was a favourite with the vicarage children. Daddy was quite good at mending toys, but George was better. He had a way with clockwork cars and engines, and he even mended dolls. The vicarage toys had a long lease of life through his strong, clever fingers.

They all sat in the car, and found they fitted nicely. The two children bounced on the back seat, but Belinda didn't mind. She liked these friendly people. 'I hope they buy me,' she said to herself.

George opened the engine lid. 'Now, Belinda,' he said, 'show the Vicar what you can do,' and he started her up.

'Belinda,' said John. 'Is that her name?'

'Yes,' said George, 'a regular little lady she is. Just listen how sweetly she sings.'

Belinda was feeling quite well now and her engine hummed happily.

John ran round to Susan. 'She's got a name,' he said. 'It's Belinda.'

'Belinda? How lovely! Mummy, did you hear what John said? She's called Belinda. Mummy, listen to her humming, just like a bee. Mummy, do look at Belinda, what does she remind you of?'

Susan and her mother walked all round Belinda looking at her from every angle. Belinda began to feel shy; she had never had so many people looking at her at once before.

'John,' called Susan. 'What does Belinda remind you of?'

John thought for a minute. 'I think she's like a beetle,' he said at last.

'A beetle,' said Mummy. 'Well done, John, because that's just what these cars are called.'

'Yes,' said Susan, 'she's just like those ladybirds we find in John's room in summer time.' And the two children joined hands and danced round chanting:

'Belinda the Beetle,
The Beetle, the Beetle,
Belinda the Beetle,
What fun we're going to have!'

Belinda was listening to this. She liked these people. She liked the way they said her name. She liked the little song the children sang about her.

'Gracious me!' said Mummy. 'Here we are making plans all about Belinda, when we don't know that we can afford to have her. How much would Belinda cost, Mr Whisker?'

'£800, Mrs Exel.'

'£800,' said Mummy thoughtfully. 'And then there'll be road tax.'

'No, Mrs Exel, the £800 includes that.'

'Do you really mean it?'

'Yes, of course.'

'Excuse me a minute, while I speak to my husband.'

Mummy scooped Daddy away from George and the engine. They went away and talked quietly for a moment.

'This is splendid,' said Daddy, coming back. 'I'll pay you now if you like, William.'

'Thank you, Vicar. I'm very pleased indeed for you to have Belinda. I don't mind telling you that two other people are very interested in her, but I don't trust them, and they certainly wouldn't give her a good home like you will. Now I can put "SOLD" on her windscreen, and choke them off.'

'How soon can we come round and collect her?'

'We'll have her painted and ready for you Thursday morning.'

'Splendid! You'd like to come and live with us, wouldn't you, Belinda?'

'Yes please, sir,' said Belinda. And no one who heard her happy humming could doubt that she really meant it.

4   Beside the sea

Belinda bumped down the sandy track to the beach.

It was Thursday morning. The vicarage family had collected her from Mr Whisker and had gone to spend their day off at the seaside, near Urlsburgh.

Belinda was feeling smart in her new coat of red paint.

'That was a lovely run,' she thought. 'Mr Exel drives so nicely, it's no trouble to get along with him.'

Daddy parked her in the shade of some bushes where she could be out of the sun and watch the beach.

'There you are, Belinda,' he said. 'How's that?'

'Lovely,' she whispered happily.

The children scrambled over the side. They couldn't wait to get out of the door. 'Wait a minute you two,' said Mummy; 'everybody must carry something. John, you take the towels, Susan, the sandwiches and books, Daddy and I will bring the rest. Right, off you go.'

'Goodbye, Belinda,' waved the children.

'Goodbye, goodbye,' called Belinda.

She felt very comfortable. The bushes gave her nice shade from the sun. She watched the family splashing in the water and listened to them laughing. 'Nice people, nice people,' she murmured drowsily, and fell asleep.

Snoop and Brown parked the big Bentley out of sight of the road. Then they walked to the turning, and saw Belinda.

'Come on,' said Snoop. 'What are you waiting for?'

'Too risky,' said Brown; 'they'd see us in a minute.'

'What of it?' said Snoop. 'There's only a parson, a woman, and a couple of kids. We could soon settle them.'

'Cut out the rough stuff,' ordered Brown, 'and use your head for once. Listen, that parson's a soft-hearted chap, he falls for any hard-luck story he's told. I'm going to tell him one, and we'll get

27

that car, search it, collect the jewels and let him have it back before they want to go home. We get what *we* want, he gets his car back, everybody's happy, and no one the wiser. What more do you want?'

Snoop grunted. 'Sounds loopy to me. How can you talk a chap into letting you have his car?'

'You wait and see. My plan's a whizzo. I'll just nip back and arrange things. You stay here and keep watch. I'll be back in an hour.'

Brown walked to the big car and drove away.

Snoop sat in the bushes. He was uncomfortable. He didn't like bushes, there were too many insects. He felt one drop down his back. He wriggled and scratched and slapped, but it still crawled about, tickling. Every time he wriggled and scratched, he made himself hotter. The hotter he got, the thirstier he became. Snoop looked at Belinda. He wondered if they had left anything to drink in her.

'No harm in looking,' he said to himself.

He crawled carefully through the bushes. Then he had an idea. 'Why not look for the drink and look for the jewels as well? If I find them,' he thought, 'I shan't have to share with Brown. I'll be well away before he turns up.' He raised his head cautiously, then, keeping low he crept over to Belinda.

Belinda woke with a start.

'Whatever's this?' she said. 'Have the children come back?' She looked towards the beach. 'No, they're still there, and Mr and Mrs Exel too. Who's poking me?'

'Help! Help!' she called, but they didn't hear. They were making too much noise with the children.

Now Belinda was a clever little car. She remembered what she had done in the garage to play tricks on people who poked her about.

Her sides were low. Snoop was tall and thin. He had to keep himself well down to avoid being seen and he found it very awkward.

Crash! Belinda's folding seat came down on his pet corn. He bumped his head and scraped his knuckles on levers which Belinda somehow managed to get in his way.

'Ha ha ha!' she chuckled.

Snoop was not at all happy. He began to think that he would have done better to wait.

'Daddy,' called John, 'there's someone in Belinda.' Snoop heard the voice and peeped over the side. He saw them looking in his direction. He slid through the door as quickly as he could, but quick as he was, Belinda was quicker, and her door slammed before he could get his fingers out of the way.

'Ow!' said Snoop.

'That's got you,' chortled Belinda. 'Serves you right. Just wait till Mr Exel comes.'

But Snoop didn't wait. Before they could get out of the water and run up the beach, he released himself and slithered into the bushes where he lay out of sight, mournfully sucking his fingers.

He watched the family come up to Belinda.

'You're right, John,' said Daddy. 'Someone *has* been here. Look at the footmarks.'

'He's been turning over the cushions,' said Susan. 'They're in a dreadful mess.'

'Look, he's pulled out the back,' said John.

'And poked about in the pockets,' said Mummy.

'Still, there's nothing missing,' said Daddy. 'That's a mercy. I'll take away the key, and we'll push Belinda a little nearer to us.'

30

But Belinda's wheels began to sink in the sand, so they left her where she was.

Snoop watched them from the bushes.

'Never mind,' said Mummy. 'We don't want to have to dig her out before we can start for home. You've got the key, Daddy, so no one can run off with her.'

'Can't they just!' thought Snoop to himself. 'Lady, you've given me an idea.'

'Come on,' said Mummy, 'we've got Belinda safe, let's have dinner, I'm famished. Susan and John, wash your hands, they're filthy.'

There was comparative silence while dinner was eaten. At last, even Susan and John had no room for more, and they lay back comfortably in the sand.

'We are having a lovely time,' said Susan, 'with Belinda and bathing and everything. We've had an adventure too, with someone poking in Belinda. Wouldn't it be fun if we could detect him like "The Famous Five" and catch him.'

'You couldn't catch anybody,' said John. 'You can't catch me.'

'I can.'

'You can't. I always hear you coming.'

'You don't.'

'I do, and Mummy says you're like a herd of elephants coming downstairs.'

'I'm not.'

'You are.'

'Well, anyway,' said Susan, deciding to ignore this insult and let her imagination run away with her, 'if I was to go to those bushes and look in them, I bet I should find something important, and I'd show it to Daddy, and Daddy would show it to the police, and they'd find out who it was with it.'

'Bet you couldn't.'

'Bet you I could. I'm going.'

'No,' said Daddy firmly. 'I'm not having either of you playing in those bushes where we can't see you.'

'But I wouldn't be playing,' said Susan indignantly. 'I'd be detecting. I want to detect. Can't I detect, Daddy, please?'

'You can go and detect in Belinda if you like.'

'But, Daddy, I've detected in Belinda. I want to go and detect in those bushes where John saw the man.'

'No, Susan,' said Mummy. 'Daddy's said "NO" and that's enough.'

Susan looked poutish and threw stones crossly at a rock.

John lost interest. He was making railway lines in the sand with a stick. 'I'm going to make a castle,' he announced, 'with towers and a moat and everything – are you coming, Susan?'

'No,' said Susan.

John, quite unperturbed, ran down towards the sea and started playing by himself. Susan pretended to be uninterested, but presently got up and ran down to join him.

Daddy and Mummy settled comfortably in the sandy armchairs they had hollowed out. For a little while they talked about the person who had poked in Belinda, but they could make nothing of it.

'Anyway,' said Daddy, 'she's close by. I don't

see that she's valuable enough to be worth steal-
ing. I expect it was a child looking at her.'

'That's it, I expect,' said Mummy drowsily.
Presently they were both asleep.

5 Belinda is awkward

Snoop lay in the bushes. He wiped his face with a handkerchief. He was hot, hungry, and thirsty, and he had all sorts of sore places where Belinda had bumped, and grazed, and pinched him.

Voices came to him from the party on the beach.

'Come on, let's have dinner, I'm famished.'

He heard the exciting crackle of paper, as sandwiches were unwrapped, and his mouth watered.

He heard the lovely cool gurgle of drinks being poured out of bottles. 'I could do with some of that,' he moaned.

'Just like Brown to leave me here starving,' he grumbled. 'I bet he's having a slap-up dinner himself. It'd serve him right if I did snitch the car and the jewels. Better not, I suppose. I'll give him another half-hour.'

The fact was that Snoop was afraid of Brown.

The time passed slowly, and Snoop, tired of doing nothing, wriggled closer; but a high treble voice brought him up short.

'Well, anyway,' said the voice, 'if I was to go to those bushes and look in them, I bet I'd find something important, and I'd show it to Daddy, and Daddy would show it to the police, and they'd find who it was with it.'

'What pests kids are,' complained Snoop, and crawled quickly away. He began to feel that he had spent most of his life popping in and out of bushes. 'All kids should rest after dinner. Their parents should insist on it. That's the trouble with these modern parents. They're too easy-going.'

The voices died away to a murmur.

After a little while he raised his head and peered out.

'False alarm,' he thought. 'Parson and his wife are quiet now. Where are those kids? Running down to the sea? Good. If Brown comes soon the coast will be clear. I'll give him ten minutes.' And he settled himself down as comfortably as he could.

'Confound it,' he said. 'What's biting me?' He

got up and turned to look where he had been sitting.

'Jiminy Christmas! It's crawling with ants.' They were scurrying in hundreds up his leg and into his trousers. He took his trousers off and flapped them furiously to dislodge the ants. 'That settles it,' he growled. 'If Brown thinks I'm going to stay here to be eaten alive, he's got another think coming. I'm going to take the car.'

Belinda was dozing.

'Thank goodness Mr Exel frightened Snoop away,' she thought. 'He is a horrid man. But I taught him a lesson, I did. I taught him two lessons. First time I pinched his head in my bonnet,' she chuckled. 'And this time I pinched his fingers in my door.

'All the same,' she went on comfortably, 'I'm glad Mr Exel took my key. I feel safer now.'

Belinda was mistaken.

Snoop crawled towards her. He still had ants in his pants, and they were still biting him. He was so cross that he didn't care tuppence about Brown. Bending double, he sprinted the last few yards between the bushes and Belinda, and scrambled in.

His fingers hurt where Belinda had pinched them, but he could still use his other hand. He took a hairpin from his pocket. He always carried hairpins. He found them useful.

He bent it, and poked it into the keyhole of Belinda's switch.

'Oh! Oh! Oh!' protested Belinda. 'Go away, you horrid Snoop!'

But no one heard, and at last Snoop found the right shape for his hairpin and turned the switch.

'I'll have to push her, I suppose,' he said to himself. 'The engine'd make too much noise.' So, getting out, he went to Belinda's front, and started to push her backwards up the track.

Poor Belinda tried to call out; but she was switched off and couldn't make much noise. 'I'll be awkward,' she said to herself. 'Perhaps if I'm awkward enough Snoop will get cross and make a noise, and Mr Exel will come.'

The track was steep, and Snoop couldn't push and steer properly at the same time. Belinda wobbled her steering wheel, and went from side to side. Every few minutes Snoop had to stop, pull her straight, and start pushing again.

After about the sixth time, he stopped to rest and light a cigarette. 'Confound it!' he muttered. 'Are we never going to reach the road?'

'Not if I can help it,' chortled Belinda. She slipped her hand-brake, and started rolling down the hill with Snoop in pursuit.

'Ha ha!' she laughed.

But the track was rough, and she hadn't got very far before a stone caught one of her wheels and stopped her.

Snoop pounced on her triumphantly. 'Drat you!' he exploded. 'Anyone would think you were alive.'

After that he was careful, and chocked her wheels whenever he stopped to rest.

'Bother that stone,' grumbled Belinda. 'If it hadn't stopped me I could have run right down the hill to Mr Exel, and woken him up.'

Then she had an idea. 'If stones can stop me

going down,' she thought, 'stones can stop me going up. Here are some. Ah!' and she settled down comfortably, with her front and back wheels wedged between two big ones. Snoop pushed and pulled frantically, but she wouldn't move.

'Hurray!' she chortled. 'That's wozzled you, Mr Snoop.'

But Snoop wasn't beaten yet. He heard a shout from the beach. He had to get away, and didn't care now how much noise he made. Scrambling into Belinda, he started her engine, and eased her over the stones.

Belinda shuddered. 'Heeeeeeeeeeelp!' she tooted.

Snoop jumped. He hadn't meant to blow the horn.

'Help! Help! Help!' wailed Belinda. 'Oh, my poor wheels and springs,' she groaned; for Snoop was racing her over the last fifty metres of bumpy track which led to the road.

'Mr Exel! Mr Exel! Help! Help!' wailed Belinda. 'Oh, it's too late,' she sobbed. She heard her family shouting behind, but Snoop had turned left, and was driving her at top speed along the coast road.

'Oh, dear! Oh, dear! Will Mr Exel ever be able to find me?' she wondered. 'I must do something to help him. What can I do? I know,' she said after a moment, and waited for her chance.

40

They came to a village. The road was narrow here between the houses, and there was a sharp bend.

A farm cart, drawn by a horse, was plodding through the narrow gap. Snoop tried to pull out and pass; but cars were coming in the other direction and he had to draw back.

'Confound that cart!' he said angrily, and he tooted Belinda's horn to make it get out of the way.

'Tooooot!' shouted Belinda. This was her chance and she made the most of it. They passed the cart; but Belinda wouldn't stop tooting, and they flew through the village with her horn blaring.

People came out of their houses, children ran after her, the horse in the farm cart took fright and bolted into a field, the policeman at the crossroads shouted, but Snoop was past caring what he said.

At last they were clear of the houses. Snoop stopped with Belinda's horn still sounding fiercely. He got out and cut a wire. There was silence. Snoop mopped his face.

'Why do these things happen to me?' he groaned. 'It isn't fair.'

Belinda chuckled, and thought about the next thing she could do.

They started again. Snoop wanted to throw the Vicar off the scent, so he swung right at a

41

crossroads. 'That will diddle them,' he chuckled. 'They'll never believe I turned back towards Urlsburgh.'

He drove Belinda hard, to make up for lost time. Belinda didn't like this. Presently, 'SsssSSS,' she hissed, and began to sway from side to side. Then bump, bump, BUMP. Snoop got out. 'Well, for evermore! It's a puncture now!'

Several people came by. They gave him advice. Snoop thought he would be better without it and told them so. At last he finished changing the wheel and started again. The road was getting

lonely, and the wind blew cold across the moors. There was not a house in sight.

'Just the place,' thought Belinda, and she began to cough.

Then she went on as if nothing had happened, coughed again, picked up, coughed again and stopped.

'Well of all the . . . ' fumed Snoop. He was so angry that he got out and kicked Belinda. He forgot that he was wearing thin shoes. He didn't hurt Belinda a bit, but he hurt his own toes dreadfully. He hopped about, holding his foot and saying things about Belinda.

But Belinda only laughed.

Snoop tried to undo Belinda's petrol pipe and blow down it, but the spanner kept slipping and he burnt his fingers on the hot engine.

'You wait till Mr Exel comes,' chuckled Belinda.

At last, Snoop gave it up and began to look for the jewels. He was in such a hurry that he pulled everything out and flung them on the side of the road, but he found exactly nothing.

He took out his knife to rip up the cushions, but he saw a big Bentley coming.

'That's Brown,' he said, and pocketing the knife, he dived into the bushes.

6 On the trail

But meanwhile, what had been happening on the beach? Daddy and Mummy were fast asleep till a bus came droning up the road. Daddy opened his eyes and reached for his book. He lay reading comfortably. From time to time he heard a scuffling noise, but took no notice. He thought the children were playing close by.

The noise went on and he glanced down towards the sea. The children were there, so they couldn't be behind him. He looked round. To his horror, he saw a man pushing Belinda up the hill. Belinda was stuck and he was trying frantically to make her move.

'Hi, stop!' Daddy shouted. He jumped up and ran along the track.

The man saw him coming, leapt into Belinda and drove her off.

'Stop! Stop!' yelled Daddy, and ran. But you can't run fast with bare feet on a stony path, and by the time he reached the road, Belinda was out of sight.

Mummy arrived a few minutes later, followed by Susan and John.

'Poor Belinda's stolen,' wailed the children. 'We did love her so.' And they began to cry.

'Never mind, my dears,' panted Daddy, out of breath. 'Just let me get some shoes on, and I'll get the police. They'll bring her back.'

'Police?' said a voice behind them. 'What's the trouble?'

They turned and saw a respectable-looking man in a brown suit.

'Somebody's stolen Belinda,' sobbed the children.

'Belinda?' asked the man. He was puzzled. 'Has someone kidnapped your sister?'

'No,' said Daddy. 'We have a little car which we call Belinda, and someone has stolen it. I saw him driving away.'

'Did you see what he looked like?' asked the man in the brown suit.

'Yes, he was tall and thin, with a hat and dark side whiskers.'

Brown's face was grim. (Did you guess the

stranger was Brown?) 'So that's who it was,' he growled. 'I might have guessed that Snoop would have something to do with it.'

'Why?' said Daddy in surprise. 'Do you know him?'

'To my sorrow,' answered Brown. 'His mother's a respectable hard-working woman, and my wife thinks a lot of her. To please her, I've employed Snoop myself, and given him every chance; but he's let me down time after time. I've spoken to him, his poor old mother has spoken to him, my wife has spoken to him. Each time he's said to me, "Mr Brown, I promise I'll go straight." But he's weak, and there are those who lead him astray. But now,' said Brown fiercely, 'he's gone too far. I'll get my car and we'll go after him and catch him.'

'But,' said Daddy, 'oughtn't we to tell the police?'

'No,' said Brown firmly. 'By the time we've answered all their questions, Snoop will have got clear away. Besides, if Snoop ever got into the hands of the police, the disgrace of it would kill his poor old mother, and my wife and I would hate that to happen.'

'Perhaps you're right,' said Daddy doubtfully. 'I'm much obliged for your help,' and he hobbled down to the beach to find his shoes.

When Brown came back with the car, the same

big Bentley, Daddy was waiting anxiously by the roadside.

The family were there to see him off.

'I wish I could come detecting with you, Daddy,' said Susan. 'Can't I come, Daddy, please?'

'No pet, you and John stay with Mummy and go back home by bus. Goodbye, Mummy dear. Don't worry, we'll find Belinda.'

'Goodbye goodbye, bring her back safe, Daddy dear.'

It wasn't difficult to discover which way Belinda had gone. Everybody remembered the sound of her horn at the first village.

'She went along the road to Castle Dredcar, over the moors,' they said.

So they forked right at the crossroads, and soon began to climb. Brown drove hard, and the powerful car sailed up the hills like a bird. Round a bend to the right they swept into a little moorland village. Here they were halted while cattle crossed the road.

A policeman with his bicycle stood nearby. On an impulse, the Vicar lowered the window and spoke to him.

'No, sir, I haven't seen a little red car BLN 111. Stolen, is it? You and your friend are trying to catch up with the thief, are you? Which way did he go? Along this road to Castle Dredcar? I see. Right you are, sir.'

Brown fumed with impatience while the constable wrote the particulars in his note-book.

'By rights,' said the constable, 'I ought to ask you to come along to the station with me and make a proper statement, but seeing as you're in a hurry, sir, I'll just trouble you to sign these notes, then I'll telephone the stations along the road, so's you'll get help.'

'Thank you, officer. I'm most grateful.'

The last cow passed, and they drove on. Brown was silent for a while, then he burst out furiously, 'What did you want to bring the police in for?'

'Look here, Brown,' said the Vicar. 'Whose car has been stolen, yours, or mine?'

'Yours, of course.'

'Very well. I'm most grateful for the help you're giving me, but I want to do all I can to get it back. If a theft isn't reported to the police, how can they

49

be expected to help? Now don't bring up Snoop's old mother. You can't go on letting him get away with it, as you say he has done in the past. It would be better for him, and for her, too, if he was stopped.'

Brown drove on faster than ever. Tyres screamed as they shot round a bend at sixty miles an hour. The Vicar shuddered, for there was a sheer drop on his side of the road. 'Steady on, Brown,' he protested.

'We can't afford to go steady,' Brown snapped. 'You and your police. We must get there before they do, that's all.'

The Vicar was puzzled. 'There's something strange going on,' he thought.

At last a straggling village came in sight. The Vicar looked at the map. 'Crossroads here,' he said. 'We'll have to inquire.'

Brown checked the car and they were waved to a halt. 'Another dratted policeman,' he muttered.

'Are you the gentlemen looking for a car BLN 111, painted red?'

'Yes,' said the Vicar. 'Have you seen her?'

'No, sir, but Jim Tabbs here was coming home from Urlsburgh and passed her on the road. She was stopped, he says, and the driver was changing a wheel. That right, Jim?'

'What was the driver like?'

'He was tall and thin, sir. There was a soft felt

50

hat on the road beside him, and he had a bristly growth of whiskers coming down to his chin, as if he hadn't shaved properly. He'd hurt three fingers of one hand and couldn't use his tools. I got off my old bike and offered to help him friendly-like, but he swore at me, so I left him and came away.'

'Thank you, Mr Tabbs, he's the man we're after.' The Vicar looked at the map again. 'He's on the road to Urlsburgh, there are no side turnings for seven miles, so if he's been held up by a puncture we should catch him.'

'Come on then.' Brown drove like a demon for the next few miles, till in the distance they saw Belinda standing with someone working furiously at her.

'What the dickens is he doing?' exclaimed the Vicar. 'Is he looking for something?'

'Looks like it to me,' said Brown grimly. 'And he's found it too.' For Snoop saw them coming, put something in his pocket and ran.

Snoop had really only picked up his knife, but Brown thought he had got the jewels.

7   When thieves fall out

Brown stopped behind Belinda. Then jumping out, he chased into the bushes after Snoop.

'Strange fellow,' the Vicar thought, but he was more interested in Belinda than Brown. She stood by the roadside looking like a skeleton. Cushions, seats, canopy, bonnet flaps, everything that could be moved had been pulled out and thrown in a heap.

'My poor Belinda, what's he been doing to you?'

'Oh, Mr Exel,' she sobbed. 'I *am* gug-gug-gug-lad you've come. S-S-Snoop *is* a horrible man.'

'Why has he pulled you to pieces?'

'He wanted to find some jewels, Mr Exel.'

'Jewels!' laughed the Vicar. 'Did he find any?'

'I don't know, Mr Exel, he's taken such a lot of

things. Mr Exel, I feel so uncomfy Mr Exel, please put me right.'

'Yes, Belinda, of course,' and he set to work.

'Jewels in Belinda,' he thought. 'How absurd! And yet I don't know. Yes, I've got it, there must have been something valuable that Brown knew about. That's why he didn't want the police. That yarn about Snoop's old mother was all my eye.'

Belinda felt better. She began to laugh.

'Stop it, Belinda,' the Vicar grumbled. 'I can't put in these screws when you shake like that.'

'Oh, Mr Exel,' she chortled, 'it was funny,' and she told him about the tricks she had played on Snoop.

The Vicar laughed. 'Well, Belinda,' he said, 'you're a clever little car, but don't you dare play those tricks on me. Do you hear?'

'No, Mr Exel, I'd never play tricks on you,' she said virtuously.

'I'm not so sure. Did you say you stopped with a cough?'

'Yes, Mr Exel, there was something in my petrol pipe.'

'Right, we'll settle that,' and he undid the pipe and blew down it. 'My goodness, Belinda, you are choked up. I'll have to get the pump.'

The tyre pump did the trick, and soon bubbling noises sounded from the tank.

But it was an awkward job, needing several

hands! The Vicar would have been in difficulties if the constable and Jim Tabbs hadn't arrived on their bicycles and helped him.

'Thank you very much,' said the Vicar, as Belinda's engine came to life. 'She's battered, but she'll go. Have you seen Brown?'

'Brown, sir?'

'Yes, the chap I was with in the big car. He went chasing after Snoop. I don't trust him much. I think we'd better find him.'

'Right, sir,' said the constable. 'Will you stay and look after the Reverend's car, Jim?'

A rough path led through the bushes into a wood. At first the constable and the Vicar heard nothing, then they approached a small clearing. Angry voices came from it.

' . . . and I tell you, you have.'

'No, Brown, straight, I haven't. I searched that darned car from top to bottom and didn't find a thing.'

'Do you expect me to believe that, you double-crossing twister. 'Course you've found the jewels. 'Course you've hidden them somewhere so you can come back and swipe the lot. But I'll not stand for that. Come on, where are they?'

'I haven't got them.'

'O.K.,' said Brown. 'I've warned you.'

There was a thud and a cry. The constable and Vicar ran forward. Snoop was whimpering on the

ground, with Brown standing over him. The constable seized Brown and the Vicar took Snoop.

'Huh,' sneered Brown. 'Calls himself a parson, does he? Fine parson he is. I help him find his stolen car, and he brings a copper and gets me nabbed. That's the fellow you ought to arrest, steals a car and £5,000 worth of jewels. I had noth . . .'

'You . . .' snarled Snoop.

'Less of it,' said the constable mildly. 'Keep your noise till we get to the station.'

They marched the two men to the road.

'We'll have these two beauties in the back of the big car,' said the constable. 'I'll drive. Jim, will you sit in with them and keep them quiet?'

'It'll be a pleasure,' said Jim. He looked big enough to keep anybody quiet.

'Now, Reverend, would you kindly help tie our bicycles on the back, so that we can get home afterwards? Thank you, sir. Now will you follow in your car and watch out for any funny business? We shall need you at Urlsburgh police-station too, to charge these fellows. And if you don't mind, I expect they'd like to have a look at your car as well.'

So it was arranged. Belinda watched, and so did the Vicar, but Snoop and Brown didn't try to escape. They sat sullenly quiet the whole way, and were handed over to the police at Urlsburgh with no trouble at all.

8   Lots of argument

It was all over at last and the Vicar brought Belinda home to Arlstead Vicarage. Mummy was on the watch and helped him put her away.

'I know you're tired, dear,' she said, 'but I did promise the children that you'd come and see them when you came in. They're so anxious about our Belinda Beetle, and I'm dying to know what happened too.' Daddy looked longingly at his supper.

'I know what we'll do,' said Mummy, 'we'll put it on a tray and you can eat it in Susan's room while you tell us all about it.'

Daddy gave Mummy a hug. 'What a splendid Mummy you are,' he said.

Susan sat up when her parents entered. John

came in in his dressing gown, and perched on the foot of the bed, and Mummy sat between them to discourage arguments. But she needn't have bothered, because the children were too interested in what Daddy told them about Snoop and Brown trying to find jewels in Belinda.

'I expect,' said John, 'that that was what the man I saw was trying to find.'

'I think so too,' answered Daddy.

'Did they find the jewels?' asked Susan. 'Did you see them, Daddy?'

'No, Susan, I didn't. Snoop said over and over again that he didn't find them, and I think he's telling the truth, but Brown is quite sure that Snoop did take them. He thinks Snoop hid them in the bushes when he saw us coming.' Daddy took a deep drink from the cup on his tray. Storytelling was certainly thirsty work.

'The police pulled Belinda to pieces again at the station,' he continued, 'and looked everywhere they could think of, but they didn't find the jewels. Belinda was very cross about it.'

'Poor Belinda,' said Mummy.

The children bounced excitedly. 'Oh, Daddy, may we look tomorrow? What fun if we find the jewels. Please, Daddy.'

'You can look if you like,' said Daddy, 'but . . . Here, I say, steady on!' For both children jumped off the bed and gave him a simultaneous hug to the great danger of the plates and dishes on his supper tray.

Presently order was restored, and both children were back on the bed.

'You'll have to be good children, mind, and not get in my way, because I shall have to work hard to get Belinda into shape again.'

'We'll be good, Daddy. Really we will,' and the children looked too angelic for words, sitting together on the bed.

'What fun it'll be,' said Susan, 'if we find the jewels!'

'And now,' said Daddy, finishing his last mouthful and draining his cup, 'it's time you were both in bed and asleep.'

John got up obediently. 'I should think,' he said solemnly, 'that the jewels are in a special secret place. Good night, Daddy.' He kissed him. 'I'm going to think of secret special places all night.'

'Good night, John. I'll come and tuck you up in a minute.'

'And as for you, young woman, bed's the place for you too,' and he picked Susan up and tucked her in.

Susan's arms wriggled out of the sheets and went round Daddy's neck. 'Good night,' she whispered. 'Thank you for bringing our Beetle back safe.' Next moment she was fast asleep.

Belinda woke up in the Vicarage stable, feeling cross. It was dark and she couldn't see properly in the dim light coming under the door.

'It's really too bad,' she grumbled. 'Mr Exel promised to come first thing in the morning, and here I am waiting hours and hours and he hasn't come yet. Snoop was bad enough,' she went on, 'but Mr Exel did make me comfy after him, and then all those policemen pulled me to pieces again. It isn't right. Looking for jewels indeed. They didn't find them neither,' she chuckled. 'Nor no one will unless I let 'em. They're *my* jewels. They were given to *me* and they're *mine*.'

She heard a scuffling outside the door.

'I can't reach it, Susan, you try.' There were some bumping sounds as if someone was jumping to reach the latch. But nothing happened.

'I know,' said Susan's voice, 'there's a box over there, John. You get it, and we'll stand on it.'

John went off, and Susan called through the door, 'Hullo, Belinda, are you there? We wanted to come and see you before, but Mummy wouldn't let us come and see you till we'd done our jobs. Have you been lonely? Daddy's coming when he's finished his letters. John's getting a box so's we can open the door. Hurry up, John, you've been ages. Now I'll get up and open it.'

'No, Susan, it's my box. I'll open the door.'

'I'm taller than you, I can reach.'

'It's my box, Susan, I fetched it. I bags first try.'

'I bagged first try while you were gone.'

'That's not fair, Susan, you can't bags things when I'm not there. You know you can't.'

'Yes, I can.'

'No, you can't.'

'Anyway,' said John, 'it's my box, I fetched it. If you don't let me have first try, I'll take it away and you'll have to fetch your own, so there. Then I'll stand on my box while you're fetching yours.'

Susan, outmanœuvred for once, had to give in and the box was put in position, with much panting and scuffling.

'Anyway,' said Susan, determined to have the last word, 'bet you can't reach it.'

'I can,' said John, and jumped up and down. 'There,' he said in triumph as the latch clicked. The door opened a little way, but they both had to pull hard to open it wide enough to get inside.

'Hullo, Belinda, we've come to see you.'

'Hullo,' said Belinda.

'Belinda, we've come to find the jewels.'

'What!' said Belinda indignantly. 'Another of them! Can't you leave a car in peace? First Snoop, then those policemen, now you. Go away. They're my jewels. They were given to *me*.'

'Oh, Belinda, have you really truly got some jewels?' asked Susan. 'How do you know you've got jewels? Have you seen them?'

'No,' said Belinda grumpily, 'I haven't.'

'How do you know then?'

"Course I know, silly. When a car feels something funny where she oughtn't to feel something funny, and when people can't leave her alone and keep poking her about in a way that no one ought to poke a respectable car about in, then that car knows that the something funny that she feels where she oughtn't to feel something funny,

is the jewels that they keep poking her about for.'

The children were quiet for a moment while they digested this piece of logic.

'Oh, Belinda, where do you feel funny where you oughtn't to feel funny?'

'Ah,' said Belinda, 'that would be telling, that would.'

'Oh, Belinda, we do love you so much. You're

such a nice little Beetle car. Belinda, please tell us.'

'No,' said Belinda. 'They're my jewels, they were given to me when I had my accident, and nobody's going to have them only me. They're mine.'

'Won't you let us peep at them, Belinda? We won't poke you, Belinda, really we won't.'

'No.'

'Oh, dear,' said Susan. 'Belinda's cross.'

"Course I'm cross. You'd be cross if you'd been poked about like I've been poked about, by people looking for my jewels.'

Susan was almost crying with disappointment.

'Belinda's all cross and horrid,' she said. 'Let's go away and leave her, John.'

'Come on,' said John, and they went out of the door.

'Here, I say,' called Belinda. 'Aren't you going to make me nice and tidy and comfy?'

'No,' said Susan. 'You're cross, and we think you're horrid.'

'Come back,' said Belinda. 'I'm not cross really. I'll let you peep at my jewels if you make me feel comfy again. I want to be swept out and polished,' she went on. 'When you've swept out and polished me, then you can peep at my jewels.'

'Do you really truly promise?' asked Susan.

'Really truly promise,' said Belinda.

64

'Oh, thank you, Belinda,' and the children ran
to fetch a dust-pan and brush, and some rags.

'No poking, mind,' said Belinda when they got
back.

'No, Belinda, we won't,' but all the same they
took things out and looked underneath.

'You're poking,' Belinda would say from time
to time.

'No, Belinda, we're not poking, we're sweeping.
We have to lift things out to sweep the dust, and
make you feel comfy.'

'All right,' said Belinda grudgingly. 'You've
swept enough now. I feel all scratchy and sneezy.
Now polish me.'

'You'll let us peep at the jewels, won't you, Belinda?'

'Time enough when you've polished me,' grunted Belinda. 'Look sharp now. I want to be polished nice and shiny.'

'But how do we polish you?'

'How do you polish Belinda?' said a voice coming down the path. 'Get a bucket of water. Then one of you wipes the dirt off with a wet rag, and the other rubs the cleaned bits with a dry rag.'

'Oh, Daddy,' said the children, 'Belinda's got the jewels, but she won't let us see them till we've swept and polished her. We've swept and now we're going to polish.'

'Splendid,' said Daddy. 'Run along and get the water.'

'Tell me, Belinda,' he said. 'Have you really got some jewels?'

'Yes, Mr Exel.'

'Where are they?'

Belinda said nothing. She went a little redder than usual, and swayed gently from side to side.

'Never mind, Belinda, I understand. You don't want to tell me so that the children can find them themselves. Is that it?'

'Yes, Mr Exel.'

'All right, Belinda. Hullo, here they come. We'd better have you outside so that they can see what they're doing.'

The two children appeared, staggering along with a bucket slopping between them. They reached the stable yard just as Belinda, pushed by Daddy, rolled out into the sunshine.

They dumped the bucket by Belinda and started arguing as to who should use the wet rag.

Susan claimed it because she was the elder.

'I bags the wet rag,' said John. 'I fetched the bucket.'

'Who had to pump and pump to fill it?' countered Susan.

'That will do,' said Daddy laughing. 'I never knew such a pair as you for arguing. Let's have a look at you. John, you're the wetter, you'd better have the wet rag first, and then, if you start at Belinda's front, you can change over when you get to her back. Off you go!'

9   A piece of string

'Oh dear, my arm does ache,' said Susan. She had been working very hard, and Belinda's paint shone beautifully where she had polished it.

'My goodness, Susan, Belinda will be pleased. I can almost see my face in it,' said Daddy. 'Good girl, that's the steering wheel side nearly finished. Not much longer now and then you can slosh as much as you like.

'John, you look as if you'd fallen in the bucket.'

John grinned. He had been enjoying himself immensely. He rested, while Susan polished the last bit.

'Change over now,' said Daddy.

Susan sloshed vigorously. 'We haven't seen the jewels yet,' she said.

'No,' said Daddy, 'nor have you finished the car. I expect you'll find them presently.'

John was rubbing with great concentration. He kept looking at the bits that Susan had polished and then going on to make his bits shine as much as hers. This made him slow and Susan had finished sloshing by the time he got to the door on Belinda's passenger's side.

Susan was dreadfully disappointed. 'We haven't seen the jewels yet and I've looked very hard. Have you seen them, John?'

'No,' grunted John. He was kneeling on the ground polishing the lower part of the door. 'There's some dirt here, Susan. You haven't washed it.'

'Yes, I did,' said Susan indignantly. 'I washed all under there.'

'No, you didn't,' said John. 'Come and look.'

Susan looked. 'That's not dirt,' she said scornfully, 'that's a bit of string, silly.' She gave it a pull. It started to come away and then stuck. 'We can't leave it like that,' said John. 'It spoils my nice polish.' He gave a hard pull and it came away. 'That's funny string,' said Susan. 'Let's show it to Daddy.'

'Daddy,' said John, 'here's some funny string we pulled out of Belinda.'

Daddy took it and looked at it. 'That's not string,' he said. 'It's leather. Where did you find it? Show me.'

'It was peeping out from there,' said Susan. 'I pulled it and it stuck, and then John pulled and it came.'

'Between the lining of the door,' said Daddy thoughtfully, 'and the frame – I wonder – Susan fetch me a screwdriver and pincers, please.'

'What for, Daddy?'

'I think you and John have found the jewels.'

'Found the jewels. Yippee, yippee,' and she scrabbled excitedly in the tool-bag.

Daddy opened the door and felt the lining. 'Yes,' he said, 'I think there's something there. John, fetch that piece of paper and put it here. Good, that's right. Now you and Susan hold the door steady while I work on it.'

Very, very carefully, using the screwdriver and pincers, Daddy prised the inside lining from the bottom of the door. There was a plop and something fell through on to the paper. It was a small wash-leather bag. Daddy picked it up. 'Yes,' he said, 'that string you found went through the hem at the top of this bag to fasten it.'

The children weren't bothering about the string. 'Daddy, the jewels. Can we see the jewels, please?'

He turned the bag upside down. A diamond necklace and three brooches fell into the palm of his hand.

'The jewels! The jewels! We've found the jewels!' The children hopped up and down with excitement.

'Yes,' said Daddy, 'you were detectives after all. You found the string which wasn't string, and that was a clue, because it told us where the jewels were.

'Now run off up the house, both of you, and tell Mummy we've found the jewels, and ask her to telephone the police. Can you remember to ask her specially not to say what we've found? I want to surprise the sergeant.'

'Oh, Mr Exel, you aren't going to give my jewels to the police, are you Mr Exel? They're my jewels, the man gave them to me at my accident.'

'Look, Belinda. The man who gave the jewels to you was a thief. He had taken the jewels from someone else. If people keep jewels that are stolen, and don't give them to the police, they have to go to prison. You wouldn't like that would you, Belinda?'

'No, Mr Exel.'

'Very well then. You be a sensible car and perhaps when the policemen give them back to the person they belong to, the person they belong to might give you a present for being a clever car and taking care of them so nicely.'

'Oh, Mr Exel, do you think they would?' asked Belinda, delighted.

'Yes, but only if you're a good car.'

Mummy came running with John and Susan. She was as pleased and excited as the children were.

They pointed proudly to the jewels in Daddy's hand.

'Mummy, look, there they are,' said Susan.

'Isn't it exciting, Mummy? John and I did the detecting. We found a clue and showed it to Daddy, and Daddy knew what it was and found the jewels.'

Mummy picked up the necklace. 'Ooh!' she said as it shone and sparkled in the sunlight with all the colours of the rainbow – 'How gorgeous, and the brooches too, one sapphire and two rubies. Oh, I do love sapphires!' and she took the sapphire brooch and turned it over and over in her hands.

'Morning, Vicar,' said a voice from the gateway. 'I got your message, and came along at once, seeing as Mrs Exel said it was urgent. What's the trouble?'

Daddy grinned at him. 'Do you remember, Ted, how you told me last week that you wanted to transfer from Arlstead because you thought it was dull here and nothing ever happened?'

'That's right, sir, and no more it does. It's just the same . . . '

'Take a look at that, Ted, will you, and then tell me that nothing ever happens.'

The sergeant's eyes nearly popped out of his head. 'The Eldbridge diamonds! Well I'll be ding dong danged! I really will, sir. We've had a description circulated to all stations, and we've been after them for weeks.' He pulled out his note-book and thumbed the pages over. 'Let me see,' he said, 'there was a diamond necklace . . . and . . . and . . . yes, that's it, two matching ruby brooches and one sapphire. Here are the two rubies, but where's the sapphire, sir? Didn't you find it?'

'Loo . . . ' said John and Susan, but Daddy shushed them firmly.

'I regret to say, Sergeant,' he said gravely, 'that you have caught my wife in the act!'

The sergeant looked puzzled.

Daddy pointed towards Belinda, trying hard to keep a straight face.

Mummy had pinned the sapphire brooch to her dress, and was twisting and turning into all sorts of attitudes in front of Belinda's tiny driving mirror, trying to see how it looked. She was quite absorbed, and hadn't even heard the sergeant arrive.

'Oh!' said the sergeant, and winked at Daddy. 'It's a very serious offence, madam,' he said, matching Daddy's tone, 'the receiving of stolen property, very serious indeed. I must ask you to accompany me to the station.'

Mummy spun round sharply. 'You're quite mistak . . . ' Then she saw their faces. 'Oh!' she said. 'Oh, all right, Sergeant. It's a fair cop. I'll come quietly.'

Then they laughed and laughed.

'I think you're awful, all of you,' said Mummy at last when she could speak.

'Never mind, we'll come and bail you out.'

Mummy protested that neither she nor the children were fit to be seen in the police-station or anywhere else. So while they went to tidy up, Daddy showed the sergeant where they had found the jewels and then took him into the house to wait.

At the station, they looked at the official

description, and saw that they really had found the Eldbridge jewels. Then they told the police all about their adventures with Snoop and Brown the day before. Daddy and Mummy signed the statement, and Susan and John wrote their names too.

'We'll get these back to Admiral Eldbridge today, sir, and I expect you'll be hearing from him soon.'

10   The full story

The sergeant was right. Admiral and Mrs Eldbridge invited the whole family to spend a day the next week at their home at Rookwood, and Mummy was specially asked to allow the children to ' . . . come in their oldest clothes, so that they can run wild and enjoy themselves with our grandchildren, Joan and Philip.'

When at last the day came, the four children had a simply lovely time. They rode the quiet, good-tempered old pony round the paddock till he felt tired and went on strike. Then they climbed trees, stuffed themselves with apples, played cops and robbers, did acrobatics on the swing, and, in short, were very happy getting thoroughly dirty. They had a picnic dinner in the garden, but were warned that they would have to come up to the house and get clean for tea, as a special visitor was coming, who wanted to see Susan and John.

So when the time came and they were as clean as their mothers could make them, they went into the drawing-room where the visitor was.

'This gentleman,' said the Admiral, 'is my friend, Inspector Sandson. He's very kindly come to tell us what we all want to know: how my wife's jewels came to be in Mr Exel's Belinda, and he also wants to meet Susan and John, who, as he put it, "beat his own men hollow at finding clues".'

This speech made the children feel rather conspicuous and shy, but the inspector came and sat on the sofa between them and talked in such a friendly way, that they were soon telling him all about Belinda the Beetle, how they found the string which wasn't a string and how that helped Daddy to find the jewels.

After tea they went and introduced him to Belinda. The inspector spoke so nicely to her, that she decided she did like policemen after all, and she didn't mind a bit when he looked at her door, put his hand in the pocket, and found a crack which he showed to Susan and John.

'There's a small crack in the bottom of this pocket,' he said. 'When the burglar was trying to hide the jewels, he pushed them in the pocket. He must have pushed so hard that the bag, being small, went right through. It was only when the string became untied and started to work through between the door and the lining that anyone like you, with sharp eyes, could see it, and find where the jewels were. I know the whole story now, thanks to you two. Shall we go in, because I've promised to tell the others too.'

When they were all settled in the drawing-room again, the inspector told them how three men, Brown, Snoop and Crib, had decided to burgle the Admiral's house, while he was away.

'They thought it would be easy to burgle an empty house, but a constable came round on patrol soon afterwards. They got away, but he called a police car to chase them. While the constable was waiting for the car, the burglars had reached the road. Brown thumbed a lorry while the others hid. When the lorry stopped, they tied up the driver, left him behind, and took his lorry. The police in the car found the driver lying on the roadside, and he told them how many men there were and where they went. In spite of that, the lorry would probably have got away, if it hadn't been for little Belinda.

'The road was narrow,' went on the inspector, 'with a bank on one side and a ditch and hedge on the other. Crib was driving very fast. Belinda was ambling quietly, driven by her former owner. Crib soon caught up and tried to pass without slowing down. There was just room, but the lorry was wider than other cars Crib had been used to, and he grazed Belinda, forcing her into the bank on the left. He tried to pull clear but swerved too far, and the right-hand wheels of the lorry went into the ditch. Snoop and Brown were flung out of the back through the hedge into a field. Crib had the jewels with him in the driving cabin. He managed to get out, nip round the back of the lorry, and before climbing the bank in an effort to escape, he stuffed the bag containing the jewels into Belinda's pocket. Her owner knew nothing of Crib's action as he was still dazed from the accident. Crib hoped, perhaps, that if the jewels were found in Belinda, the police might think that Belinda's owner had stolen them, but though Crib was caught, the jewels, as you know, weren't found till last week.

'Snoop and Brown saw Crib put something in Belinda, but it was so dark they couldn't see where it went. Now you know why Snoop and Brown were so interested in her, and yet couldn't find what they wanted. We have got all three of them now, so they won't trouble anybody for some time.'

'Thank you, Inspector,' said the Admiral. 'By the way, that young constable did a good job when he tackled those three ruffians in my house. Judging by the state of the room, he must have had a pretty tough fight. I'd like to give him a present, just to show appreciation.'

'I'm sorry, Admiral, but that would be against regulations. I've got my eye on him, and he'll probably get promotion before long. If you care to write me a letter though, saying how much you appreciated his work, I'll see that it goes where it will do the most good.'

'Thank you again, Inspector, I'll do that. Now we come to the moment to which Mrs Eldbridge and I have been looking forward all day.'

He smiled at his wife and she twinkled back at him, and they looked for all the world like a pair of mischievous children.

Everybody wondered what was going to happen next, for the old people had kept it a close secret. The Admiral cleared his throat.

'We can't show appreciation to the constable, but we can to our other friends here. The Exel family have come on what we hope is going to be the first of many visits, and we have enjoyed their company very much indeed. John and Susan, we've got a surprise for each of you in the hall. Go and see what it is.'

The children ran out and came back flushed and excited.

'Bicycles! Are they really for us? Oh, thank you, thank you!' and they gave the old lady and gentleman such hugs, that they beamed with pleasure and cried for mercy both at the same time.

'May we go and try them?'

'Of course you may,' and away they went, followed by Joan and Philip.

Then the Admiral gave Daddy a present. It was a 'repeater' watch which pinged out the time when you pressed a knob. While he was saying 'Thank you', Mrs Eldbridge went to Mummy and fastened the sapphire brooch to her dress.

'No, really,' said Mummy, 'thank you very,

very much, but I don't deserve a valuable present like this. I didn't find the jewels, you know.'

'Maybe not,' smiled Mrs Eldbridge, 'but if it hadn't been for you, my dear, there'd have been no John and Susan to find them for us, and where would we have been then?'

Everybody said 'Hear, hear!' and gathered round, telling Mummy how well the brooch

suited her, till she was so pleased and happy that she didn't know what to say.

'That's that,' beamed the Admiral. 'Now, we mustn't forget Belinda. Come on, all of you,' and he led the way to where Belinda was standing outside the front door.

'Belinda,' he said, as he took a tissue paper parcel out of his pocket, 'I've got a present for you.'

'Oh, sir! Thank you, sir! Is it a really truly jewel?'

'No, Belinda, it's not a really truly jewel, because if bad people like Snoop and Brown saw you with a really truly jewel, they might want to take it away, and that would never do.'

'No, sir,' said Belinda.

'But even if this isn't a really truly jewel, it shines and sparkles like a really truly jewel, and you can wear it on your bonnet for always. Then everybody who sees it will know you're an "Extra Special Car", and they'll say "There goes Belinda the Beetle".'

'Oh, thank you, sir!' said Belinda happily, 'that will be lovely.'

Then the Admiral unwrapped the 'jewel', and Daddy helped him fasten it on Belinda's bonnet, and when the jewel was there, all the colours of the rainbow seemed to be there too. They all admired it and told Belinda how nice she looked, and the Admiral said, 'Three cheers for Belinda the Beetle,' and led the cheers. Belinda was very pleased and proud.

Belinda chugged home that evening with four very happy, tired people. She was sorry she was too small to take the bicycles as well, but the Admiral said never mind, he'd bring them in the truck tomorrow.

When her master put her to bed in the stable, she was so happy that she kept on singing the little song which she had made up on the way home. Belinda found it went best to the tune of *I Love a Lassie*. She called it *Belinda's Jewel Song*, and she sang it softly till she fell asleep.

Here it is:

'I've got a Jewel!
My very own Jewel!
A Jewel that was given to me.
It's better than the other, which was really
*   quite a bother,*
And my Jewel's one all can see.

I've got a Jewel!
Belinda's own Jewel!
A Jewel you all can see.
I'm an Extra Special Car, 'cos you'll search
*   wide and far,*
For a car with a Jewel like me.'

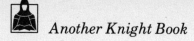

Another Knight Book

Rev W Awdry

BELINDA BEATS THE BAND

When Belinda, the little red Volkswagen Beetle, is run off the road by a big lorry, it doesn't take long for Bert, her new friend at the garage, to mend her. Then Bert disappears mysteriously, kidnapped by a band of dangerous criminals; can Belinda and the children find Bert and beat the band?

MORE GREAT BOOKS AVAILABLE FROM KNIGHT

ROLF HARRIS
☐ 39223 1 Your Cartoon Time £2.99

ENID BLYTON
☐ 54875 4 Five on a Treasure Island £2.99

WALTER FARLEY
☐ 19687 4 The Black Stallion £2.99

JUDY CORBALIS
☐ 40860 X The Wrestling Princess £2.99

RUBY FERGUSON
☐ 04136 6 Jill's Gymkhana £2.99

ANDREW MATTHEWS
☐ 54722 7 Mallory Cox and His Magic Socks £2.99

DAVID TINKLER
☐ 50166 9 The Scourge of the Dinner Ladies £2.50

REV W AWDRY
☐ 58007 0 Belinda Beats The Band £2.50

All these books are available at your local bookshop or newsagent, or can be ordered direct from the publisher. Just tick the titles you want and fill in the form below.

Prices and availability subject to change without notice.

HODDER AND STOUGHTON PAPERBACKS, P.O. Box 11, Falmouth, Cornwall.

Please send cheque or postal order for the value of the book, and add the following for postage and packing:

UK including BFPO – £1.00 for one book, plus 50p for the second book, and 30p for each additional book ordered up to a £3.00 maximum.

OVERSEAS, INCLUDING EIRE – £2.00 for the first book, plus £1.00 for the second book, and 50p for each additional book ordered. OR Please debit this amount from my Access/Visa Card (delete as appropriate).

Card Number ☐☐☐☐☐☐☐☐☐☐☐☐☐☐☐☐

AMOUNT £ . . . .

EXPIRY DATE . . . .

SIGNED . . . .

NAME . . . .

ADDRESS . . . .

. . . .